Civil Twilight

Simon Fruelund

Translated from the Danish by
K.E. Semmel

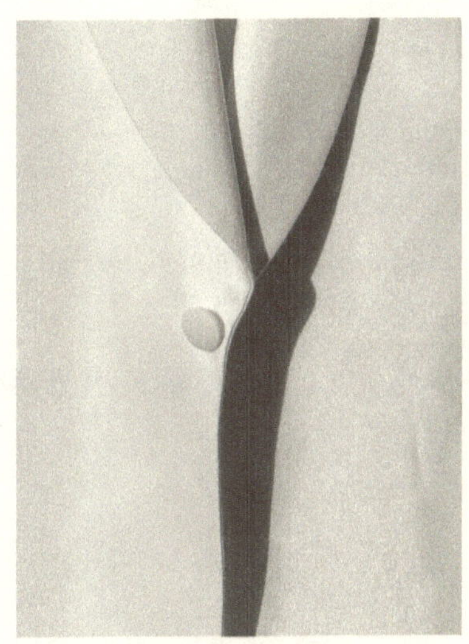

SPUYTEN DUYVIL

New York City

Special thanks to The Danish Arts Foundation for financial support towards the translation and publication of this book.

Cover design by Camilla Hultén Fruelund

Library of Congress Control Number: 2024943740

The Street:
Dante's Allé

1

Sitting in church on Sunday mornings, she sometimes thinks of what her husband once confided to her:

As a young man he dreamed of becoming an actor.

He looks suddenly so authoritative.

His diction is so clear.

He performs the rituals with a barely perceptible, practiced hesitation, with a restraint that reasserts a bit of the drama.

His homilies are full of exclamation points.

She's secretly happy that his parents talked him out of becoming an actor.

If there weren't a clear and unambiguous script, she isn't sure he would be able to withstand his own charm.

He is six feet five inches tall.

He has lightly frizzy dark hair.

He is very eloquent.

She's a professional singer, but restrains herself a little when they're singing the psalms.

She has no desire to be in the spotlight.

She has no desire to upstage the parish clerk and his wife.

2

Paving stones have been arranged in the gravel to mark the parking spaces, ten feet between spots.

In the summertime, the gravedigger goes over the lot with a weed torch.

3

It's a nice little house with a gable roof, and the widow who lives here never wears black. It doesn't bother her when the vicar's wife practices her singing. Nor does it bother her when the church bells toll. Not because she doesn't hear well; she's simply learned to ignore such things.

There are rhododendrons in her garden.

There's the weekly bridge game.

There's the young man who mows her yard.

4

A conservator is in full swing restoring the church frescoes. She fills in the cracks and freshens up the color.

There are small devils who lead each other by the tail and a depiction of Abraham and Isaac on the mountain.

She has never seen a Jesus look so Danish.

He has pink cheeks and a little belly.

5A

When the flight attendant returns home late at night, the neighbor's cat is often waiting for her.

She heard once that cats have a mirror behind their retinas. That's why they see so well in the dark, why their eyes glow.

She's having an affair with a married man.

His semen tastes a bit like garlic, and he is allergic to cats.

He's developed a pill for diarrhea called Propitin.

The neighbor's cat loves shrimp.

5B

They have a greenhouse made from old windows.

The youngest boy loves to sit inside it. He removes all his clothes if it gets too warm.

His father has seen him sitting buck naked in the center, drawing lines in the loose earth.

The lines resembled letters, but nothing he'd ever seen before.

—How do you spell "idiot"? the boy once asked the cat.

He told his wife, the boy's mother.

She doesn't think there's any reason to be concerned.

6

Here lie the dead.

7

They've grown too old to travel, but sometimes she puts on a dress and says to him:

—Do you remember this one?

—Rome?

—Tenerife.

He puts on a pale suit and sits in the car waiting.

They drive to the airport, and he straightens up as they enter the doors. They sit at a café in the departure area.

She drinks a glass of white wine, he drinks a beer.

They watch the many travelers check in and go up the escalator in their freshly ironed clothes.

They reminisce about the places they've been: Harzen, Madeira, Egypt, etc., and after an hour or two they drive home.

He used to be a locksmith.

She used to be a nurse.

Some Sundays they go to church.

8

Sitting on the toilet in the first-floor bathroom, he can see the cemetery. He's often seen the cat from across the street hunting mice over there or lying on a stone in the sun.

He's in tenth grade and during the day his parents are almost never home.

Sometimes he thinks about the flight attendant. In his room he can tell when she comes home at night. One time as he mowed the widow's lawn, she'd lain topless in her yard.

He fantasizes that he'd gone over to her.

Every now and then he's seen a green Jaguar parked at her place.

9, first floor

He owns a motorcycle, a 1968 Triumph, and he's a member of a club called Pegasus Motor Club.

Their logo is a depiction of a white horse with wings. They're part of the opening parade at Bakken Amusement Park and each summer they ride to Skagen.

When he delivers the mail, he does it with a bicycle. His route is on the opposite side of town.

He doesn't believe a person should mix work and play.

9, second floor

She's not quite comfortable with her downstairs neighbor. She raises her ten-year-old daughter on her own, and even though he seems relatively harmless, she doesn't like the way he transforms.

He walks differently, slower, with a bowlegged gait whenever he wears his leather clothes.

What does that have to do with poetry? she wonders.

And what kind of image does it give her daughter about the male gender?

The girl's father, a famous American anthropologist, has long since returned home to Milwaukee.

10

The house was built in 1901, and he has renovated it himself.

He has laid new tiles and replaced all the windows. He has built a carport.

He's happy with his handiwork, but wishes his house was just a little farther down Dante's Allé.

He's tired of the chiming bells, especially when there's a wedding.

When he was a young carpenter's apprentice and got married at Copenhagen's City Hall, times were different; there wasn't so much of that stuff.

Once, he talked to the vicar at a block party.

He was friendly enough, but something just wasn't quite right.

—He has a tail, he told his wife later.

11

They are both teachers. They have two children, an eight-year-old boy and a five-year-old girl. When the mailman kickstarts his Triumph, the boy runs to the window.

One time when they came home from the city there was a whole row of motorcycles parked across the street.

They stood watching.

A middle-aged woman in leather came out and sat on a blue Yamaha. Next came an older gentleman with a full gray beard. Then came the rest of them. Around twenty in all.

The boy stood with a gaping mouth and watched as they rolled away.

12

She's forty-seven and a personal care assistant. Her husband is a gardener and employed with the county, just as she is.

She cleans at the widow's a few times a week and also at the retired professor's down in number 18. Sometimes, when she scrubs the floor, he comes over with a piece of candy balanced on a spoon.

Maybe it's because he spills on his shirt every now and then, or maybe it's because of the terrible smell that she cannot clean out of the house, but it requires an immense effort for her to open her mouth.

He's lonely, she thinks, letting him extend the spoon onto her tongue.

13

The engineer's wife dreams of a man in a white suit.

He's walking down Dante's Allé.

He's tall and trim.

The suit, which fits him perfectly, follows his movements in delayed little swishes.

He has friendly eyes, white teeth, wrinkles that flatter him.

14

The man who lives here has nothing against foreigners. He's a rehabilitation specialist. One case he worked on was that of a brain-damaged Turkish boy who'd spent his first years living with dogs.

The family that has moved into #19 is Indian, he knows.

They've lived here about one year.

At the block party they stood off by themselves.

He was on his way to welcome them to the neighborhood, but the engineer offered him a Belgian beer, and soon afterwards they were gone.

They have four children, and he has two.

They're not in the same class at school.

His girlfriend says that she greets the wife whenever they meet in the supermarket.

15

There's a little tower on the house. It has a copper roof and a spire and a little dragon weather vane.

The house is divided into two floors plus a basement.

He's a retired police chief, and she's been a secretary at the same company for nearly thirty years.

She hopes to continue working until she's sixty-seven.

He's read an article in the local newspaper with the headline: "10,000 killer snails captured in house garden."

They come from the South, the article says, and that doesn't surprise him.

16

She's a biochemist and employed by Novo.

He's a lawyer.

When there's a full moon, she can't sleep.

The moonlight makes the photographs of her relatives on the wall look like ghosts.

The chair where his clothes lie neatly folded suddenly seems so foreign to her.

His mustache twitches just slightly.

He sleeps heavily.

Typically she gets up and goes into the living room.

She sits in a chair with a book.

Often she reads until the children wake up.

That's how she read Isabel Allende and Kirsten Ekman and Helen Fielding. She's also read Dostoyevsky and Jane Austen and Henry James.

In the small hours of the night she has often seen an older man in a white suit amble past the house.

17

A For Sale sign has been posted and already some people have come to see the house.

According to the ad, the house is "a genuine and charming villa in red bricks with plenty of light and a delightful, mature garden."

—I think they're interested, said the wife afterwards.

—Of course they are, her husband said.

When they first met, she told him about a man from Sæby with extremely large feet.

For some reason he thinks about him quite often.

18

The house needs a loving hand.

He gets help for the garden, and also the housecleaning, but the windows are chipped and the sills are cracked.

He's a retired professor and likes mint and chocolate drops.

His wife is buried in the tomb of the unknowns.

Usually he goes there on Sundays, but not to church.

Every so often a large black cat visits him, and he reads aloud to it.

He has read Ovid to the cat, *The Art of Love*, so that it purred.

19

She was trained as an accounting assistant and he as an astrophysicist. They were born and raised in Delhi.

They've lived on Dante's Allé for a year and a half and in Denmark for fourteen.

He drives a taxi, and she manages the business they own. They have a fleet of fourteen Mercedes and one minibus.

If there's ever a problem with the union, she expects him to handle it.

If there's a meeting with the taxi driver's association, it's also his to deal with.

Usually he drives the night shift and gets out of bed when the kids come home from school.

He recently drove the neighbor's wife home from the city. He saw her kiss another man before she climbed into his car.

As they neared Dante's Allé, she gradually became friendlier.

When he meets her now, she always smiles.

20

Sometimes her parents talk about the Indian family across the street. They talk about house prices, and then they talk about "those people over there." When they pass them on the street they greet them politely, but there's something about her father's smile and the glance he gives her mother afterwards that tells her she'd better keep quiet.

Here are the things everyone knows:

They own a Volvo.

They emigrated from India.

They paid nearly five million kroner for their house.

Then there are the things she knows:

Their house smells funny.

The living room wallpaper is pink.

They watch strange movies with singing and dancing and colorful costumes, and the youngest daughter gets all dressed up and dances in front of the TV.

There's a large closet in the basement filled with old clothes, and when you feel the silk against your bare legs, you get goose bumps.

They have a PlayStation 2.

After they moved in, her parents began to go to church.

21

The yard is overgrown.

Her son refuses to do anything about it, and she refuses to hire someone to do it.

Her son is thirty-seven and lives at home.

Wild roses grow here, small birch trees, and an elder bush where once there'd been grass. It took only a few years, and now the problem can't be fixed with a lawnmower or a scythe.

It has been twenty years since her husband left her for a younger woman.

It has been five years since she fell and hurt her back.

Her son has three unfinished degrees; he's now a substitute in an after-school program.

She supports herself by ghostwriting other people's books.

This year she's written three autobiographies, one for a women's handball player, one for a politician, and a third for a businessman who owns his own jet.

In the book about the businessman, there's a photograph of his wife and a famous American actor. They're standing in front of a huge casino in Monaco; it was taken some time in the early '70s. The actor is wearing a tight yellow shirt with very large collars.

There's something about that photograph.

She has discovered that a fox lives in her backyard.

22, first floor

Even though they only have the ground floor, they've got enough room. The two small rooms that face the backyard are only used when they have overnight guests.

They've lived here for three years.

He's a regional manager for Danske Bank, and she's a lawyer in the county of Copenhagen.

They've received three fertility treatments at the public's expense and two at their own.

His sperm count is down 87%.

Her sister has three children and each time became pregnant on the first or second try.

All of their friends have children.

He has begun to play squash, she does yoga, and together they've taken an evening course in French cuisine. They've also learned Salsa. When she danced with the instructor, he had to look the other way.

They don't drink coffee or alcohol and they eat only organic food.

He'd never prayed to God, but of late he's begun to pray for a child.

He's recently been promoted for the second time in two years.

22, second floor

She's forty-four and a nurse. Sometimes when she comes home after a long day at work, she takes a hot bath.

Sometimes she closes her eyes.

She imagines she's standing on the balcony. It's summer and the yard is filled with sunflowers, and a tongue is sliding up her thigh.

The tongue belongs to a man, and it's not the Indian man who lives across the street.

Nor is it the mailman with his long legs.

Nor is it the high school kid with the shy demeanor or the rehabilitation specialist who helped her change a gasket.

Nor is it the vicar, because even though he's tall and dark, it's hard to take a man in a dress completely seriously.

It's not the politician's husband or the well-groomed

lawyer in number 16, but it's more likely to be him than the Indian.

The yard is filled with sunflowers and someone has raised the flag.

In spite of herself, she thinks about the Indian. Afterwards she sniffs her fingers.

She shaves her legs.

—I have nothing against foreigners, she says to her thigh.

23

It's been a long time since he has prepared a dead body himself.

He's cultivated his connections among public authorities, and slowly he's perfected his concept: a branch in each quadrant of the city, installment plans for the poorest, discounts for the rich, tactful chauffeurs, and Volvo hearses. He started at the very bottom and now he has eight branches.

He bought his villa five years ago.

He's built a discotheque for his children in the basement.

When he and his wife go to the summer cabin, he makes the local beer dealer deliver a few kegs. None of the neighbors have complained.

The only condition is that everything be cleaned up come Monday morning.

24

She doesn't like walking past the cemetery late at night. When she's on her way home from the city or from a party at the high school, she usually walks down Brydenholtsvej.

If she doesn't have the energy to take the long way home, she walks on the other side of the street.

One June night she heard sounds coming out of the cemetery. It sounded like someone singing.

A man sat on the grass just beyond the gate.

He was dressed all in white, and she gasped in pure shock.

—Hey beautiful, he said.

She ran so fast her nose bled.

25

He's employed at the Danish Refugee Council and works fifty hours a week. His wife is a Social Democrat and a member of parliament.

She's never home.

One of her core issues is organic farming.

Each week they receive a box with organic vegetables of the season, and each week they have to throw most of it away.

Their house is the biggest on Dante's Allé.

It's a white house with glassy black tiles and it once belonged to a manufacturer.

26

In the evening the crows arrive. They come shortly before sundown and settle in the linden tree.

It's as though the tree comes alive.

The man who lives here has nothing against animals. There's just something foreboding about crows.

He's forty-five and divorced.

He hoses the bird shit away, but even so, it leaves dark stains on the sidewalk and the garden path.

He's thrown stones at them, and a rubber boot.

The boot got stuck up there, so he had to borrow the neighbor's ladder the next day.

He's considered chopping the tree down.

He's considered buying a gun.

He sees his kids every other weekend.

27

There was once a time when she never would've dreamed of voting for a Social Democrat.

Her husband was a Conservative, and so was her father. But the young man next door has helped her trim the bushes, and at a block party she fell into conversation with his wife.

Since then they've regularly stopped to chat when they meet on the street, and she's asked whether they'd like to come to dinner.

It's not happened yet, but it will.

She's still mobile.

She goes to the theatre and the opera, but never to the ballet. Her husband ruined that for her.

28

They have a horse chestnut tree in the backyard, and each fall his wife gathers the chestnuts. With a towel she removes the white rind from the eye so that it doesn't rot.

She builds a bed of them on the floor and asks him to lie on it.

She blames the computer for his bad back.

He's writing a book on volcanoes.

Using various websites he follows along with measurements from, among others, Etna and Mt. St. Helens.

He says that carbon monoxide from volcanic activity played a decisive role in the origins of life.

—Close your eyes, she says. Relax.

He tries.

He thinks about a famous Danish physicist who always carried a chestnut in his pocket.

29

They've been burglarized. The thief cut a round hole in the window of a basement door but didn't leave any other traces.

The silverware and all her jewelry are missing.

Their son recently left home.

He's in twelfth grade and has moved in with his girlfriend, a twenty-seven-year-old, divorced woman with two kids.

He's just told them she's pregnant.

—You're sure it's yours?

—Thanks, Mom. Really.

She prays it's not his child.

She prays that she gets her jewelry back.

She imagines that God and "the good" are one and the same thing.

She works as a medical secretary but was educated as a commercial correspondent.

30

He's filled the garage with empty bottles, and now he's begun to fill the cellar.

Neighbors, friends, and acquaintances give him bottles.

He would like to travel to the U.S., but his wife dreams of seeing the Himalayas.

—Think about our tired old legs, he says.

—Nobody says we have to climb them. I just want to *see* them.

He shakes his head.

—Don't you hear it? she says. Himalaya, it sounds like a dream.

—What about Malibu? Or Mississippi?

—Means nothing to me.

He has a handcart for collecting around the block. Otherwise he uses the car.

He keeps a car freshener in the trunk, and he rinses the bottles with the garden hose before he brings them inside.

He believes it's good to have a hobby.

He believes it's worth the effort.

The last time the bottle deposit went up they traveled to Kenya for a whole month.

31

She once slept with a famous singer.

Her husband was in Portugal building a cement factory, and the children were away for the weekend at their grandmother's.

She and a friend met him at The Forester's Inn. They sat at the bar chatting and drinking, and when her friend left, he put his hand on her thigh.

They were both pretty drunk.

—Let's call a cab, he said.

It was dark outside, it was January.

He couldn't get it up.

She did everything she could but ended up having to kick him out before dawn.

Her friend called the next day.

—*Well?* she said.

—Nothing happened.

That was thirty year ago. When she hears one of his songs on the radio today, her face turns red.

Sometimes her husband hums along with the tune.

32

The more settled they become, the more clearly she sees just how odd he is.

He is evasive, he forgets things.

He says there are ghosts in the cemetery, but the house is not haunted.

He says the vicar should get his act together. You need a lot more than Christian values to frighten the spooks away.

—You have a screw loose, she says.

—Just wait, he says. You'll see. I'll invite one of them over for coffee someday.

Luckily he's not without his practical sense.

He has torn down the wall between the kitchen and the dining room.

He has repaired the antenna and cleaned the furnace.

He has plans to build a terrace facing south.

He's not a bad father.

33

She worries that the neighbors will see all the empty bottles, so she usually takes some down to Aldi whenever she goes shopping.

The rest, about a case a week, she gives to the Bottle Man.

Her husband works for the railroad.

He's never hit her.

34

She's a psychologist and has set up a clinic in the basement.

He's a television newscaster, and three or four evenings a week the kids can see their father on the news.

He's interviewed the Social Democrat over in number 25 a few times.

He's asked the woman in number 49 whether he could film a segment on her husband, to no avail.

He often thinks about him.

He wore light blue shirts and drove around in an Opel Astra. He was just a regular guy.

Many times, his wife has offered to have a chat with their kids.

35

He's a bricklayer, and she's a kindergarten teacher. They were married in the year 2000.

The vicar recited a poem about some butterflies, said something about Jesus, and encouraged them to be good to one another.

The wedding was held in a restaurant at the Deer Garden.

The restaurateur got a new bathroom, and they got free food.

It was the very best.

They've only been to church once since then:

When their youngest child was baptized.

The vicar is always very friendly with them.

Vicars usually drive gray cars, but this one has a silver Alfa.

They talked to his wife at the block party.

She thought:

She walks like a man.

He thought:

She's got nice boobs.

They have no problem with the gay guys next door, but generally they don't believe the church should be open to everything.

36

When the church bells toll, the child kicks. It also kicks if he lays his hand on her belly.

It's their first child.

If it was born today it might not survive.

In a book they've read that the child practices breathing by moving its chest in and out.

The book says that the child dreams.

What can an unborn child dream of?

That it drinks amniotic fluid?

That it stretches?

That it hears strange noises?

He once saw a cat bare its teeth as it slept. He knows that dogs whimper.

She's talked to a girlfriend.

—It feels like shitting a chest freezer, her friend told her.

37

They are the only male couple on Dante's Allé, but they're not the only gays.

More than once they've met the lawyer who lives in number 16 at a bar in the city.

They've lived in the house for eight years, and before that they lived in Frederiksberg.

He is a nurse, and he's a doctor.

They work at different hospitals.

They purchased their furniture at Paustian and in Casa Shop. They have a small but rare collection of art.

They give money to an eleven-year-old boy in Tanzania via The Christian Children's Fund.

On weekends they often bike up to the Deer Garden, and usually they take a detour down around Taarbæk.

They have new 7-speeds and professional cycling pants.

—One day we'll sell our Kirkeby painting and buy a house here, the doctor says.

The nurse smiles.

He's okay with the fact that it will probably never happen.

He's okay with living on Dante's Allé.

When they moved in, he bought a copy of *The Divine Comedy*.

The portrait of the long-nosed Dante and his narrow lips and grim-looking face almost made him stop reading before he'd started.

It didn't help matters that the main character cried at the drop of a hat, was struck dumb with pity, or broke into a cold sweat every time he met one of the lost souls.

After he'd fainted twice in the first ten pages, the nurse thought:

He's worse than the worst fag.

38

He delivers newspapers on weekends.

He gets up at 4 a.m. and is finished by 7 a.m.

He listens to Eminem on his MP3 player or Den Gale Pose. Sometimes he listens to Rammstein.

His route goes down Dante's Allé, Brydenholtsvej, Balzac's Allé, and Bog Drive.

Often he sees the fox that lives in the overgrown garden.

In number 43 there's a dog that barks, and in 54, once in a while, he finds a ten-kroner coin waiting for him.

Sometimes he sees a man in a white suit.

When he passes the Indians' house, he watches for their eldest daughter. She's in another class in his grade, and her hair is black and long.

When she laughs, it feels like someone has punched him in the gut.

Sometimes he passes Cervantes' Allé on his way home.

One of his friends sent him a photo of a girl. She's Czech and an au pair and in the photo she wears gym socks and nothing else.

He stops and pulls up the image on his cell phone.

His friend says she lives above the garage in number 14.

39

There is a personal care assistant who comes several times a day, and there's a nurse who comes every morning. Her daughters take turns staying with her.

She dozes off, and when she awakes another person is sitting by her side.

Her son comes all the way from Rudkøbing.

The grandchildren come too.

The eldest is a student at the architecture school and is dating a chef.

The next-eldest wants to be an actor and was recently accepted by an acting school in London.

The youngest, who's only sixteen, has begun to invite young men home.

She took a long time to get started herself, and her husband quickly lost interest.

It makes her happy to see how they dive right in.

Sometimes when she dozes off, a well-dressed gentleman is sitting at the side of the bed when she wakes up.

He's suntanned and wears a large gold ring on his finger. His clothes are white.

—Shall we go? he asks.

He offers her his arm, and they go outside.

The organ is playing, and people stand behind the hedges, smiling.

40

They have two Japanese cherry trees in their yard.

He drinks single malt whiskey from the Scottish highlands and smokes a pipe tobacco which, in spite of its English name, is produced in China.

She works for a Swedish firm and enjoys Italian food very much.

They drive a German car and have wicker furniture from Bali in their sunroom.

They vote for the Danish People's Party.

41

She's thirty-five, and he's fifteen years her senior. They've lived on Dante's Allé for four years.

He has three children from his first marriage.

Each child has a room on the first floor, but only one of them lives there.

Once in while, when she comes home late in the evening and sees the house bathed in light, she thinks about something they experienced in California.

There was a guesthouse at a big Victorian mansion. They went inside to ask about availability, but the reception desk and lobby were empty. Instead, the room was teeming with teddy bears in every imaginable color and size.

They looked at each other and hurried out.

42

Stuffed in a desk drawer on the second floor is the bullet that nearly killed him.

His studio is on the first floor.

He photographs young girls in designer clothes. He photographs kitchens, furniture, and food. He's taken over two hundred shots of the same car: a Skoda Octavia.

He doesn't travel anymore.

About a year after the episode with the bullet, he was walking down Dante's Allé.

There was a loud bang and he leaped into someone's backyard.

The engineer was cutting bushes.

—Are you okay? he asked.

He glanced down the street and saw that a truck had just placed a large open container by the curbside.

43

She's seen them more than once. Usually it's on the weekend and during summer.

A group of middle-aged men and women in leather riding a variety of motorcycles.

They slow down a bit just before they cross the small speed bump in front of her house.

One of the women is a little chubby; most of the men have beer bellies.

A few of the motorcycles are not much bigger than mopeds.

The dog barks when they ride past.

They don't look like Hell's Angels, but they wear some kind of insignia.

She understands the charm of riding a motorcycle. But why be a member of a club?

Wouldn't it be more fun to choose your own speed?

She'd once had a lover who drove a scooter.

They made short trips north in the summer, usually to Hornbæk or Liseleje.

44

He knows everything about elephants.

His little brother just started playing soccer and is already on the first team.

His big sister spends over an hour in the bathroom each morning and won't let them come into her room.

Besides humans, elephants have no enemies.

When they die, they die of hunger because their last pair of molars are worn down.

He knows there were once elephants in Denmark.

He imagines them walking down Dante's Allé: straight-tusked elephant and woolly mammoth.

When the funeral director comes out to see what's going on, the mammoth picks him up with its long tusks and tosses him up over the hedge.

The Bottle Man leaves his handcart and runs into somebody's yard.

Trees are ripped up, cars stomped flat.

The fight attendant screams.

The Indians get on their knees in their front yard.

The windows vibrate.

The earth rumbles.

A whole herd has arrived.

The mailman tries to save his motorcycle.

The vicar's wife lifts her blouse and flashes her breasts.

He himself stands in the middle of the street waiting.

Just as the elephants are about to trample him, he blows his whistle.

They stop.

They scrape their feet against the asphalt.

He blows his whistle again, and the first elephant drops to its knee so he can crawl up on it.

The elephant stands.

He gives it a little pat and the herd ambles down Dante's Allé.

Many of the houses are destroyed.

Trees grow through roofs, and wrecked and rusty cars sit in carports.

Where the road ends, the forest begins.

45

His father drank a glass of schnapps with his lunch. On weekends it often became a few more.

His mother read palms and believed in everything between heaven and earth.

His deceased wife was obsessed with shoes.

For many years following her death he continued to find shoes around the house: on the furnace, in the lowest kitchen cabinet, behind the wood pile—even the freezer.

Their eldest son likes red wine.

The youngest married a vegetarian.

He frequently sits at the window in the big recliner.

From here he can see the house across the street with the handsome mansard roof.

From here he can reach his cigars.

46

On summer evenings, when he's out in the yard, he hears her laughter now and again.

She's not beautiful.

She's a few inches taller than he.

She walks in a funny way, as if there's something wrong with her hips, and she sometimes forgets to close her mouth when others are singing.

Still, he has stood behind a pine tree in the yard of the vicarage and spied on her.

One time he followed her silver-gray Alfa all the way to Køge.

In his car he keeps a little lunch box filled with CDs that she's recorded.

He often manages to see the same production four or five times, and usually he sits up in the front.

He can tell she's noticed.

He has seen how her eyes scan the front rows as she walks on stage.

More than once in each performance, he's seen her look directly at him.

He's seen her furious and near death from exhaustion.

He's seen her humiliated and euphoric.

When they meet on the street, they greet each other briefly.

He fancies that she smiles at him in a special way.

47

His mood swings up and down.

When he's down, he's impossible to drag out the door.

When he's up, he's impossible to drag home.

If it wasn't for those afternoons in the woods when he suddenly pulls her between the trees, or evenings when he turns off the TV in the middle of a film and looks at her, then she wouldn't have been able to make it.

There are worse fates.

More than once she has asked the neighbor if there was something she could do.

48

Her birthday is in May. She can write her own name, but not much else. Her mother has helped her write a wish list:

Barbie prince

Barbie house

Barbie horse and carriage

Easel

Pretty dress with roses

Stockings with red flowers

Animals: zebra, elephant, parrot, bull, rhinoceros

Her grandparents are coming. Her mother's father is dead and lies in the ground. Her friends from preschool are coming. Her mother says the weather is usually good on her birthday. Then they can be outside. Her father doesn't have to work that day. They'll have ice cream. Maybe twenty people will come.

49

She's not heard from him in eighteen months.

He drove to the store to pick up milk one Tuesday evening, and three days later his car was found at a rest stop somewhere in the south of France.

In his bank statements she can see that he's used his Visa card at the local Q8 gas station and after that a few places in Germany, Switzerland, and France. There are no traces after that.

The police have dug through his accounts.

They've interviewed colleagues and friends (did he have a lover? A secret vice? was he mentally unstable?) and registered him missing through Interpol.

She has gone through his drawers and clothes.

As far as she can tell, the only articles he took with him were his passport and his wallet.

She's written to the Foreign Legion's office in Marseille and gotten a polite, apologetic response:

Upon arrival, all Legionnaires are provided with a new identity, and no questions are asked.

—I think he's dead, their eight-year-old son says.

The girls, ages four and five, have gradually begun to forget him.

She herself has stopped running to the telephone when it rings.

The neighbors have offered to help all they can, but what can they do?

The vicar says that he prays for them.

She doesn't know what she should pray for.

50

She thinks it's embarrassing when her parents kiss each other on the street.

She thinks it's embarrassing when they hold hands.

She thinks that her father looks stupid when he smiles, and that her mother wears the most horrible outfits.

She doesn't want to be seen with them, anywhere.

She wishes they were divorced like most other parents.

Then she could live with them in rotation and go on two summer trips each year.

She thinks about the man across the street a lot.

Her theory is that he's won the lottery and thought: Well, hell. Now it's my turn.

She imagines him sitting on a beach in the Caribbean with a drink and a girl with nougat-colored skin.

51

He's the coach of the local lady's handball team, and this year he believes they'll win.

His daughter is the goaltender.

He's got to be careful not to yell at her too much.

He plays on the Old Boys' team, and his wife plays tennis.

He's a mover:

FAITH MOVES MOUNTAINS

WE'LL MOVE THE REST

They've lived on Dante's Allé for ten years.

52

When she meets the neighbor's wife, she asks her about the children or about her work. She's stopped asking about him.

There was something about him that was a little frightening.

He had everything under control.

The yard, the car, the children, the hedges, the house, his clothes, everything was always more than in order:

It was perfect.

What did he have to hide?

In the first weeks afterwards, her heart palpitated if her husband was late.

Luckily, some color has begun to return to the wife's cheeks.

53

She's a member of the local history society. She's given a few lectures to the county's elderly and at different schools. She tells the district's story.

A good number of stone axes have been found down near the bog.

When they first began constructing the villas around 1900, Bronze Age graves were unearthed.

Right behind the church that stands today, traces of a wooden church have been found that most likely burned to the ground.

There's a great deal of information in church records.

There's a report of a man who sold his soul to the devil to secure a good harvest.

There's a report of a woman who was sentenced to death after committing adultery three times.

There's a vicar from southern Denmark who writes that the residents of the village are lazy.

54

Some Friday evenings he puts out a little money for the newspaper boy.

There used to be problems with the service, but after the architect's son took over the route the paper arrives as it should.

He likes to get up early on weekends and sit in the kitchen with the newspaper and a good cup of coffee.

During the summer, he pulls back the curtains so he can see the yard.

During the winter, to avoid seeing his own reflection, he doesn't.

The furnace rumbles in the basement. Upstairs, a board in the floor creaks because someone's on their way to pee.

He turns the pages, and in between he glances out at the yard or at the curtains.

He's thirty-nine and a psychologist.

When the family begins to stir, he puts the newspaper aside and sets the table.

He gets rolls out of the freezer and turns on the oven.

55

She almost never sees him during the day.

He resembles a famous Danish composer whom she sees on TV every now and again.

During the day he's dressed in dark clothes, and in the evening and at night he's dressed in white.

She thinks it's a curious habit.

He's always tan and always alone.

She would invite him in for coffee or lunch if she wasn't too old for that kind of thing.

She has her garden, her children and grandchildren, and on Wednesdays there's Bingo.

56

From his office on the second floor he can see most of Dante's Allé. To the east he can see the church and the vicarage, and to the west Brydenholtsvej with the bog and the Mosehøj projects on the other side.

Between these two points are all the villas and their yards.

He's often considered writing a crime novel that takes place here. It should be something about a girl who's kidnapped, and a retired police chief who starts snooping around.

Maybe the girl's father is bisexual?

Maybe the police chief is repressing something from his past?

He imagines some satanic rituals and a young, charismatic vicar who leads his parish into the dark.

He himself is the principal of one of the local schools.

He's sixty-two.

When I retire, he thinks, then I'll have the time.

57

He knows there are three types of twilight.

He's been sitting in the yard during each type, hoping to catch a glimpse of their new neighbor.

The civil twilight lasts from sundown till when the sun is six degrees below the horizon.

At this point you can still read the newspaper.

The nautical twilight is from six to twelve degrees, and now the brightest stars start to show. You can distinguish between individual trees.

The astronomical twilight is from twelve to eighteen

degrees, and only when it's over can you start making astronomical observations.

—Why are you suddenly so interested in this stuff? his wife asks.

—It's good to think this way, he says. You see things more clearly.

She shakes her head as if to say, "I've never heard anything like it."

They've been married for thirty-seven years.

He's just looking.

He's seen her stand naked in the window and talk on the phone.

58

She was once an actress.

She has played Hedda Gabler and Queen Gertrude and Lady MacBeth.

Fifteen years ago, she retired and threw herself into humanitarian work.

At a conference in Miami she met a famous black singer and actor.

They fell into conversation, and when they

discovered that they were staying at the same hotel, they made plans to eat lunch together.

Since then, she's visited him and his wife in New York City on multiple occasions.

One time they came to Copenhagen.

Her sister tells her she's in love with him.

—No, she says, for God's sake.

She knows that's not the whole truth.

She is in love with him, but as one falls in love with a star:

It's not meant to go anywhere.

It's not the real thing.

It is a product.

She keeps a photograph on her wall, in which they stand together in front of the hotel.

59, first floor

She has been painting:

The bedroom is rose-pink, the kitchen is light yellow, and the rest is white.

She was given a dining table by her parents, and she bought a couch from IKEA herself.

The apartment is actually her grandmother's, but her grandmother is now in a nursing home.

She knows four people in Copenhagen.

Three of them are over sixty, and the fourth is her cousin, a royal guardsman.

She has spoken to the woman upstairs and thinks she seems nice.

She has purchased *Krak's Map of Copenhagen* and doesn't leave the apartment without it.

She's been accepted at the Technical University of Denmark and looks forward to getting started.

59, second floor

There's a balcony turned toward the southeast where, in summer, she often sits with her breakfast.

The walls are slanted and there's a bathroom with a tub from which you can look up and see the sky.

She has lived here alone the last four years, and now she has begun to search online.

It's Ana L. who gets the most responses, but it's Smiling Sussi who gets the most serious ones.

She's had eight dates as Sussi, five as Freaky Rikke, and one as Ana.

In most cases she bailed after only a few minutes.

60

He's happy he doesn't live on Cervantes' Allé.

He has read the story of the ingenious nobleman from La Mancha, and he has read *The Divine Comedy*, and he prefers the latter by a long shot.

Traitors to the Fatherland lie in the ninth circle, closest to Lucifer, with only their faces free of ice:

It's a fate worse than that which befalls murderers and despots.

He likes that.

He himself almost lost his life in the struggle against the Germans, and he has no sympathy for those who changed sides.

Don Quixote on the other hand:

To confuse a brass basin with a warrior's helmet!

To be afraid of a fulling mill!

To attack a group of monks!

That's something for cowards.

61

She's a journalist, and she's a chef.

They bought the house two and a half years ago and remodeled it themselves.

They've removed a wall and put in a new kitchen.

They've painted windows outside and inside and tarred the base of the house.

They've re-organized the yard and laid new flagstones.

They are used to hard physical labor.

When they lived on Østerbro, they were part of a group called "The Grumpy Pussies."

They worked out twice a week at the local gym and took good care of rapists, wife beaters, and pedophiles.

The neighbor, an older gentleman with a gray mustache and a slightly militant appearance, nods when they meet on the street, but he clearly avoids them.

62

She can recognize a chess player from afar. It has something to do with the way they walk and their somewhat reclusive manner.

They walk down Dante's Allé in the evening, and they're always men.

They enter the gate at number 72 where the chess club resides on the floor above the kindergarten.

Mostly they look a little unhealthy.

She hopes her son doesn't get interested in that kind of thing.

He's never said anything, but she's aware that he's being bullied at school because of his good grades.

63

Only seldom do they talk to their neighbors to the east.

It's not that they don't like lesbians; they just don't feel they have much in common with them.

The family on the other side has kids the same age as theirs, and they've cut a hole in the hedge so the kids can slip through.

They've barbecued together in the summer.

The husband works in IT and has helped them with their computer. The wife is a designer, and it shows in their home.

They themselves are civil servants: He's a consultant in the Ministry of Education, and she's a nurse.

Every now and then they discuss quitting everything and opening a small restaurant.

64

He's been eyeing the school principal's lawnmower. It's one of those you sit on, and when he sees him circle around between the trees, he thinks:

If I wasn't such an honest person.

His wife has also noticed it.

Not that they've exchanged many words about it, but her eyes get a little glassy when she sees it.

She gets that same look when they meet the neighbors in the supermarket and the wife is wearing her fur, or when they are in the yard and the doctor in number 82 drives by in his new Volvo.

They have a relatively big lawn, and now that the children have moved away, it's up to him to mow it.

It takes more than an hour.

With the principal's machine he could do it in a quarter of an hour, and he would not have to run the gauntlet in front of all the neighbors.

65

It's incredible what children can do.

If it weren't for the fact that her two boys get along so well with the neighbors' son and daughter, they'd hardly have anything more to do with them.

Her cheeks are exhausted from smiling when they return from a visit.

Is it because they always say what she expects them to say?

Is it because they always say what they think she wants to hear?

Or is it because she herself is not able to relax?

She would like to think better of them.

She feels stiff in their company.

She's tried to confide herself to the wife and flirt discreetly with the husband, but both lead only to embarrassment.

The wife started talking about a crisis they'd overcome in their marriage, and the husband winked.

He winked!

She could've died.

66

She remembers the time there was an ice cream vendor
on Main Street.

On a warm summer day she saw some firemen
standing there eating ice cream.

They had axes hanging from their belts, they wore
dark uniforms and helmets and tall boots.

They ate waffle cones, and she remembers that sight
more clearly than her own wedding.

Recently she saw an immigrant girl walking down
Dante's Allé.

It was a Sunday morning, and she carried a bag of
rock salt.

She was around ten-years-old and clutched the bag
with both hands.

She herself was on her way to church.

She cannot recall a word of the vicar's sermon, but
she keeps seeing that girl.

67

He's been a member of the church council for eleven
years and has lived on Dante's Allé for twenty.

He's read the vicar's book on Christian ethics and he's certain that in another era he would've been burned for heresy.

He thinks that sermons for children, gospel concerts, and book clubs where you read contemporary novels and poems are frivolous.

When they hired the vicar, he himself was hospitalized with kidney stones, and when he sits in the church on Sunday mornings, he often thinks about how painful that was.

68

In the mornings when the girls are in school, she turns up the volume on the stereo.

While she cleans or does the dishes, she listens to the Cure or the Smiths or Elvis Costello.

In the afternoon she writes applications.

She was trained to be a drafting technician.

Once in a while she drinks tea with the elderly woman in number 66.

Her husband was an auctioneer, and the house is filled with old furniture and a lot of art.

She's small and agile and has bright eyes.

The elderly woman gave her a monkey puzzle tree, and she's planted it so that she can see it from the kitchen window.

The branches resemble monkey tails a bit:

They stretch in every direction.

69

They adopted a girl from Sri Lanka.

She's a year and a half old, and it's almost been one year since they were in Colombo to pick her up.

Sometimes, when they meet the Indian couple from number 19, they stop and chat with them.

—Aren't you pretty, the wife usually says, or:

—Come visit us someday.

The husband says something in a language that makes their daughter smile.

—How much do you think she remembers? they ask each other later.

They know she was left at the mayor's doorstep as a newborn and then lived with a local family.

They've not met her foster family, but they know they were farmers.

She smiles when they sing, and doesn't like to have anything over her head.

She eats everything they serve her.

70

Actually, her mother has thick lips, but she has a tendency to squeeze them shut.

She can tell from her mother's mouth when it's a good time to ask for money for clothes or a trip to the movies.

When it is narrow, she resembles a piggy bank. She puts lipstick on her own lips and makes them full.

Her father's lips are neither slim nor thick, and he's not stingy.

Unfortunately he's seldom home, and all too often sides with her mother.

71

They once found an old gold ring in the yard.

A sparrow flew into one of the windows, and when they dug a hole for it behind the gooseberry bush, they saw something that glimmered.

They told the lady in number 53, and she recommended they send it to the National Museum.

A few weeks later they received a Thank You letter.

The Director of the National Treasures Department wrote that the ring dated back to the 8th century, and that it was probably made in southern Germany.

He enclosed a check for 1,200 kroner.

For the longest time they'd talked about buying new cushions for their garden furniture, and when a few days later a flyer plopped through their mail slot they weren't slow to react.

The cushions are thick and dark green, and when they sit on the patio and look over their well-trimmed yard, the lush rhododendron, and the fruit bushes down at the edge of the lawn, he often thinks:

Things are not so bad.

72, first floor
The kindergarten is in an old villa. To the north there's a smaller adjoining building, and to the west and south there's a playground.

There's room for thirty children.

The woman who cleans here is Moroccan and lives in Mosehøj.

The lead teacher lives on Balzac's Allé.

She's married to a cabinet maker, and together with some of the fathers they've recently expanded the playground with a jungle gym and a ropewalk.

Most of the teachers live in the area, and a few of them have had children in the school.

The cook is a former sandwich chef.

72, second floor

The club has nearly eighty members, but it's rare that more than twenty come on any given evening.

There are high school kids and university students, teachers and civil servants. One is an assistant professor, another is a locksmith. A few of them have psychiatric diagnoses.

In the room that faces the street they play speed chess and drink coffee. They analyze moves and discuss the Norwegian wunderkind Magnus Carlsen or the Indian Anand or the Cuban Capablanca.

In the room that faces the yard they play tournaments.

They play Spanish and English, Sicilian and nimzo-Indian, Pirc defense, and the poisoned pawn, and the only thing you hear is the sound of felt against wood, ticking watches, and an occasional "check."

73

She's in the vicar's book club.

This year they've read Tolstoy and Dickens and a few contemporary novels.

She likes it when there's a story, and you know which side you should be on.

Her husband always complains about all the books she brings with her to the summer house.

—I want a selection to choose from, she tells him.

Recently she read about a Persian caliph who brought all his books with him when he traveled.

He had more than 100,000 volumes, and they were borne by camels he'd trained to walk in alphabetical order.

74

He collects old watches.

He visits flea markets on weekends and second-hand stores during the week.

He's a former janitor, and he was born and raised here.

His father and grandfather owned a grocery on Main Street, and he keeps his collection of watches in one of his grandfather's old counters.

He has more than four hundred different ones.

He rarely speaks to the neighbors, but now and then he talks to the actress down in number fifty-eight.

He knows he was a handsome man once, and he imagines he can see that in her eyes, but what would a celebrity like her want with a nobody like him?

Sometimes, while watching soccer on TV, he plays a drinking game with his grandchild.

Every time a goal is scored in one of the thirteen matches, you've got to drain your glass.

75

There's a small fountain in front of the house.

It's shaped like a water lily, and the stream flows out in place of the flower.

She enjoys waking on summer mornings and listening to the water gently lapping over the edge.

Her husband is an insurance agent, and she's on disability.

During Christmas preparations some years ago she began to hear voices.

—You should never roast a duck higher than on 300 degrees!

—Jesus died for your sins!

—Keep your hands off the marzipan!

—That's what you get for drinking too much port wine!

As long as she swallows her pills the voices stay put.

Every once in a while her husband talks about removing the fountain, but luckily he's lazy when it comes to physical labor.

76

He has his own glider plane. He keeps it in a hangar in central Zealand, and when the weather is right, he drives down there.

His wife is Swedish and bears the name of Dante's great love.

She's never been thrilled about his hobby, but they've stopped arguing about it.

When the wire is released, and there's a little jolt to the plane, he's sometimes reminded of the shock it gave him the very first time.

When he's poised under a cumulus cloud, winding upwards in tight circles, he usually feels elated, and if for a moment he thinks about his wife it's with the serene warmth that so easily evaporates in the daily crush of small tasks and annoyances.

77

She's not a member of the Danish National Church.

She's thirty-four years old and a librarian.

They've lived in the house for four months, and their oldest child has just begun school.

He's grown close to the vicar's son, and that worries her some.

She can clearly remember how terrifying churches were to her when she was a child.

It was cold there, it smelled sour, and there was a dead man nailed to a cross.

She still feels that way, largely.

If the message was love and compassion, why have an instrument of torture as unifying symbol?

It's as if you threaten people with death and then promise redemption and eternal life to anyone who signs up.

How attractive is eternal life when it comes right down to it?

Wouldn't it be a little boring in the long run?

Isn't it good enough to be eaten by worms when nature has nourished you your entire life?

Her boyfriend thinks she's too fixated on religion, but he's long since agreed that they won't baptize their children.

They can decide for themselves.

78

He's a member of FC Copenhagen's fan club.

He's got season tickets and goes to all the matches. He drives with one of his friends who's eighteen and has a car.

He gave his friend a small white T-shirt to hang in the rear window.

It reads:

Honk if you wanna hump.

He's a plumber's apprentice and lives at home with his parents.

They've given him permission to fix up a room in the basement.

There's often a group of them down there, having some beers before heading out to the bars.

He doesn't make monkey noises, like the others do, when a Black player has the ball.

79

She's a high school teacher, and he's a dentist.

They've been married for almost forty years and have been close to divorcing at least five times.

They've tried open marriage and partner swaps and membership in a swinger's club, and still they've continued to cheat on each other.

With age they've grown calmer, but even so:

Whenever he hires a new assistant at the clinic, she

marches up there the first day to get a look at her.

The Social Democrat up in number 25 is one of his patients, and every time they drive past, he glances at the house.

Whenever they see her on television, he says:

—It's too bad she won't whiten that tooth.

Or:

—Hasn't she gained weight?

She herself once had a liaison with the janitor.

They did it on the workbench in his garage, and she remembers a sled with rusty runners hanging on the wall.

She remembers that he had a long, slightly curved penis that rammed against her cervix when he shoved it all the way in.

He was a lot handsomer back then, but no smarter:

Of course he had to tell his wife about it.

All those puppy-love looks he's given her in the years since!

80

She's been to more than one party in the funeral

director's basement, and it amazes her a bit that a person can get so rich by selling coffins.

She doesn't know anyone who has died, apart from her grandmother, and that was so many years ago that she's nearly forgotten it.

There was beer and wine and chips and a lot of candy, and upstairs there was leather and marble and steel.

There were flat-screen televisions in both the living room and the kitchen, and in one of the bathrooms there was a hot tub.

The son put his wet tongue in her ear, and she slapped his face.

The problem is that she's in love with someone in her class.

If she bikes past on a Friday or Saturday evening and hears a party, she wonders whether he's down there.

81

She goes to The Owl quite a lot. She's made a decision to never drink alone, and she keeps to that.

Her children moved away from home a long time ago.

Her husband moved out around the same time as the youngest.

She's decided to never go down there before supper, and she keeps to that.

Sometimes she talks to the man in the white suit.

He's a former Copenhagen champion Jitterbugger.

He's had his own company.

He has four children, and one of his daughters is a designer in Milan.

He's been married into a rich Italian family.

A couple of times they've walked home together.

It's quiet on Dante's Allé in the middle of the night.

He behaved like a gentleman, which was probably just as well given their age and blood-alcohol levels.

82

In truth he would've like to have become a pianist.

His daughter attends the conservatory, but he almost never touches the piano himself.

He's a doctor with a practice up on Cervantes' Allé.

Four physicians share a secretary and a nurse, and he earns around $150,000 a year curing small problems and referring patients to specialists.

His wife is a pharmacist.

She's employed at the local pharmacy, and she gets visits almost daily from middle-aged women with prescriptions for psychoactive drugs that he's written.

It's not something they discuss.

Nor do they discuss the bottle resting on the highest shelf in the garage, or the dent that has appeared on their new Volvo.

They know each other, after all.

On rare occasions she'll wake up during the night and hear him play.

83

She has a degree in Danish and History and teaches high school.

Her husband is an economist and works for a union.

They've lived on Dante's Allé for three years, and before that they lived in the city.

She misses having her friends close by.

She misses the immigrant shops.

She's joined the local history society and has been to a single lecture.

She thinks that life in the suburbs is a little too quiet, but luckily they've become good friends with the vicar and his wife.

They talk about music and politics, about people on the street, and immigration.

Their views are not radically different, but not so similar that it becomes boring.

All four of them appreciate a good debate.

84

He runs around the bog every evening, except when it's raining.

He's thirty-four and a psychotherapist.

He's married to a woman who is ten years his senior and a yoga instructor.

They have Tantric sex a few times a week and eat biodynamic food.

They rinse their noses together before bed.

They have no car and believe that the neighbor's two cars (of which one is a Mercedes) display a lack of resource consciousness.

When they met at a course three years earlier, she lived with a woman, and he in asceticism.

They bought a house with the inheritance her parents left her and designed it in accordance with Steiner and Feng Shui.

She claims she's seen a ghost more than once in the front yard.

She says it wants to tell them something important.

He hasn't seen anything but daisies and dandelions and grass that, over time, have grown rather tall.

85

"He's not displeased with himself" was one of her father's standard phrases.

He never used it in reference to his son-in-law when she was around, but she knows that he's thought it.

He talks loudly and penetratingly.

He has a big appetite.

He quotes Groucho Marx and laughs so that it resounds.

He farts with pleasure.

It startles her now and then, but more often she's delighted that he's so carefree.

He makes people around him relax.

He sails through life on a slipstream of ease.

He's not the most gifted among his siblings, but he's the one who made the most of himself.

If it was up to him, they would have moved to something bigger and more comfortable up north, but the children prefer to stay where they are.

He bought a Mercedes instead.

Why should he be displeased with himself?

He's the CEO of a business that manufactures hearing aids.

She's a speech therapist.

They've lived on Dante's Allé for fifteen years.

86

They live on the corner of Brydenholtsvej.

From time to time, when the wind blows from the west, and it is summer, she can smell the bog.

She has a sensitive nose:

She can smell a sour dishcloth at three hundred feet or wine in a corked bottle before it's opened.

The bog reeks of dead fish.

When she sits on the patio and her husband brings

the coffee and calva or maybe a glass of Bourgogne, she says:

—Oh, how nice. I'm just about to choke on this stink.

He has learned to take her comments with a grain of salt.

He can't smell anything.

He likes the bog: The soft paths, the ducks, the coots, the birch trees.

Sometimes he runs into the psychotherapist down there.

They don't talk, just greet each other.

He recently saw two young swans eating apples off the ground in one of the adjoining villa gardens.

History

Imagine two hunters who've followed a wild boar heading west.

One has brought a dog, and it has run ahead of them into the dense forest.

They've walked for more than an hour.

They've climbed a ridge, and on the way down the other side they've sensed the presence of a lake or massive bog.

One of the hunters noted a row of young elm trees in the shade of the tall lindens and, later, he returned to the spot.

He brought a large flint ax with him and he selected a tree with a circumference of four to six inches.

From the knotless tree he has carved out an almost seven-foot-long bow.

On occasion, his tribe appeared and disturbed the silence with their axes.

The years passed.

Stags, roe deer, wild boar have come and gone. A pine marten has been nosing in the dry autumn foliage.

On rare occasions, a moose or an aurochs crashed through the underbrush, but over time they've disappeared.

A young woman with a child on her back has gathered mushrooms here, and more and more regularly, hunters have begun wandering here in search of food.

One cold winter day, men from two different dwellings stumbled upon each other.

One of them was pierced in the breast with a hazel arrow, and the victorious tribe lit a fire and roasted the meager prey over it.

One spring day the forest resounds with chopping axes. A small group has settled down on the shores of the big lake. With them they bring domesticated animals, and before long oxen and long-bristled pigs are walking among the trees. They trample the new buds and eat from the trees and bushes.

Small parcels of forest are cut down and burned and the land seeded with dwarf wheat and naked barley. The soil is rich and full.

The new settlers hunt in the forest and wander to the coast when they need flint.

The soil is soon exhausted, and new glades are cleared and seeded.

A plow is built and two oxen are yoked to it.

A house resting on three tall central columns is built approximately where Dante's Allé today flows into Brydenholtsvej.

A slightly smaller house is built one hundred thirty feet away, and in a nearby clearing a grave mound is erected some years later.

Cows are milked. Cheese and junket are now produced.

From the grains they produce porridge.

Fish from the lake and wild animals from the forest supplement the diet.

People dress in wool sheared from sheep that are grazing the nearby forest into a common.

The flint knife is replaced with one in bronze.

The dead are now cremated.

Longhouses are built with fire pits at each end.

Heavily armored men on horses thunder past occasionally.

On midsummer nights sacrifices are made to the gods.

The tribes' elders throw two very large, lavishly

bejeweled axes into the water from a small boat while the others stand on the lakeshore.

The women wear large belt buckles with patterns of spirals.

The men have small ornate razors.

On one the handle is shaped like a horse's head; another depicts the sun's journey across the sky.

The climate grows colder. Beech trees now populate the common instead of linden trees.

The dwelling has grown into a little village.

The houses face east-west and stand around a communal square.

One of the houses is much bigger than the others; attached to it is a smithy and a small shed that's used to store hay.

The cows are penned inside, and their manure is carried in wooden buckets out to nearby plots of land.

Iron ore is dug up from a bog an hour's walk to the north and is carried home in oxcarts.

The smith produces daggers, axes, sickles, and scythes.

Beer is brewed from wheat and honey, and cranberries and bog myrtle are blended in.

A lone warrior brings unfortunate news to the village:

A great army has reached the country to the south.

The young men take off, and for a long time rumors swirl:

They turn free people into thralls.

They rape the women.

They are unusually barbaric.

Only one returns to tell what happened:

In a fierce battle many hundreds of men were killed, and the invading army forced the chieftain and his clan to flee.

The elderly men continue to farm the fields together with the women. In a nearby village they buy a few thralls. A few plots of land are conjoined.

The foreigners ride past occasionally on their way to the sound.

Reluctantly the townspeople offer them food and drink and water their horses.

The newcomers call themselves Danes.

The townspeople pay tribute to them once a year.

The climate grows colder and damper. The grass thrives

on meadows and commons, but many cultivated fields must be turned into grazing pastures. The beech forest expands.

Tools, stuffs, and pottery produced in the village are transported to a trading center up north, and in exchange they bring glass, bronze, gold, or coins home.

The will of the gods is interpreted in the birds' flight or the horses' manure.

They cast lots:

A branch from a fruit tree is hacked into small pieces and notched. The pieces are thrown on a white cloth, and the village's chieftain picks up one at a time, three in all, and deciphers them.

The nearby lake has become a large bog.

Here sacrifices are made to Odin.

One of the young men enlists his service to the king, and many years pass before they see him again.

In the intervening years he's learned to carve runes and he bears a large gold ring on his right hand. He tells them the king has encamped beside the fjord, facing west, and that they've built a gigantic hall where they hold great drinking fests, and thralls are sacrificed to the gods.

He gives his gold ring to one of the young women and impregnates her before he travels on.

Later, they hear that he was slain in a battle against the Angles.

Now there's a road that passes through the village.

Separate cattle sheds have been built with room for up to fifty cows.

They pray to the new God, Christ.

Following an ordinance from the king they now pay taxes to the Bishop of Lund.

They trade in Danish coins.

On a hill toward the east, a few hundred feet from the village, a small stave church has been erected.

It has been built with long, vertical oak planks, and the gable ends are equipped with carved-out dragon heads.

They use a plow that turns the earth instead of simply making furrows.

They sow in both spring and autumn.

In a village a bit to the north they dam a little brook and erect a watermill, where the grain is ground.

They've begun to bake bread.

They plant apple and pear trees.

They pay a tithe to the church.

The village is overrun by the Wends.

They plunder, rape, and burn houses down.

The mightiest farmer is crucified, and the stave church set to flames.

Young men and women are taken prisoner.

The most powerful farmer's son—who has fled to the forest—builds the church that stands today in memory of his father.

The church is constructed of granite boulders the peasants have collected over many years.

A fresco painter decorates its inside according to the son's instructions.

They live at the end of the Sixth Age and await Armageddon.

This is when Jesus will return and the seventh, eternal age begins.

They wait.

They obey the laws of the land the best they can.

They catch herring in the Øresund in August.

They pay taxes to the king:

2 marks of wheat

3 marks of malt

14 oxen

22 pigs

15 hunks of cheese

8 barrels of herring

9 crocks of butter

1 pound of salt

To mark the days of the year, they use a cane with notches.

To pass the time, the Guild Master has a game made with carved-out pieces.

There's a king.

There's a queen.

There are peasants.

When the Norsemen attack, they flee inland.

When the plague rages, half of the village's population dies.

The priest says the Jews are behind it.

He encourages everyone to fast on Fridays, confess, give alms to the poor and pay taxes to the pope.

They have a village assembly attended by landowners, and the richest is typically the Guild Master.

If anyone breaks the laws they've created, they'll have to pay a fine.

They pay in money or in beer that's consumed at lavish feasts.

In the church they now sing psalms and use a Danish bible, which no one besides the vicar can read.

During the service he quotes from the Second Book of Exodus:

"Thou shall not let a witch live."

An elderly woman in a nearby village curses her neighbor, and when he suddenly dies a half-year later, she's put on trial.

The woman is led to the gallows hill on the other side of the bog and hanged.

A woman in the village is executed later that year after thrice committing adultery.

The vicar instructs the most gifted children how to read and write.

A farmer gets his son to draft a letter in which he sells his soul to the devil.

If the devil will assure him of a good harvest, he will follow him to the end of the earth.

The letter is discovered, and the farmer is locked up.

The district bailiff sends the case on to the bishop who sends it on to the university in Copenhagen; there, the governing body sentences the farmer to death.

He escapes, however, and is never seen again.

The village now has its own cobbler.

The grain multiplies nearly four-fold.

On The Day of the Seven Sleepers, you can tell whether the harvest will be wet or dry.

If there's sun on the treetops All Saints Day, it means the coming year will be rich in beechnuts and acorns, and the pigs will flourish.

The vicar writes in the church record that the village's residents are lazy, and that their fear of God is more forced than sincere.

It consists more of words than deeds.

If they don't go to church on Sundays, they are fined four shillings.

If they can't pay the fine, they're given an hour in the stocks.

A surveyor ensures that everyone gets their due:

The farmers each get sixty acres, and crofters get small plots of land in compensation for their lost grazing rights.

A parcel of land east of the church is reserved for a school.

Most of the farms are razed and rebuilt outside the village on their respective plots of land.

Some buy their freedom; others get a copyhold.

The village now consists of three farms, a few dispersed houses, a church, and a vicarage.

They begin to cultivate clover, rapeseed, turnips, and potatoes.

A school is being built.

The teacher has a globe in his office, and he's got books on his shelf that not even the most quick-witted pupil is allowed to borrow.

The students learn Danish and basic math.

They learn of the Battle of Copenhagen and The Count's War.

They learn the creed by heart.

They learn the psalms.

They learn to honor the king and the fatherland.

They read a book called *Truth to Piety.*

They go to school only every other day.

Three of the farms are divided into parcels.

Houses sprout up on the fields down by the bog.

The village teems with horse-drawn carriages and craftsmen. Bricks are hauled in baskets and mortar churned in huge vats. A carpenter sings as he hammers nails into the beams:

The seaman, he must suffer

A lot more bad than good, good, good

Trees are planted along the roadsides, and gardens created.

The trees on the former gallows hill, on the other side of the bog, are chopped down.

Bulldozers, excavators, and cranes are brought in, and shortly after that concrete slabs on long bed trucks.

The carpenters, electricians, and plumbers arrive.

They use electric drills and hoist up building

materials using a winch. They sit in trailers parked in the mud and eat their lunches.

The architect is a tall thin man with round metal glasses.

He wears knitted sweaters and ergonomic shoes.

In the course of a few months, a shopping plaza and five apartment blocks appear.

The Project: Mosehøj

1A

He's posted a small sign on his door.

It's got a photograph of a German shepherd, and above the photo the sign reads:

Beware of Dog.

He's fifty-nine.

He's on disability, and the dog is not a German Shepherd but a Labrador Retriever.

He's lived here for four years, and before that he lived on the fourth floor in a building closer to the city.

He owns a three-wheeled moped that's parked in a locked storage room in the basement, and every afternoon he and the dog ride the elevator down.

There's a ramp that leads from the basement to the parking lot, and from there it's a two-minute drive to the bog.

It takes them about an hour to drive around the bog.

He had a stroke four years ago.

He once owned his own bakery, but for the last fifteen years he'd worked in a supermarket.

Once a week someone from the county comes to clean, but he takes care of everything else.

He's not bitter.

Sometimes he takes bread with him to feed the ducks.

Sometimes he bakes a marzipan ring when his daughter and her children visit him.

1B

She's lived here for eight months and has been clean for nine.

She's been assigned the apartment.

She visits Narcotics Anonymous twice weekly and has begun studying Danish at the local qualifications school.

She takes long walks around the area.

Typically she avoids the beautiful villas on the other side of the bog.

There are newly groomed lawns, children playing, and carports with expensive cars with their trunks poking out.

There is quiet.

She smokes forty cigarettes per day.

She doesn't drink.

She avoids the neighbors as much as she can.

What would she say if they ask?

That there are many years she doesn't remember?

That her children live with a family down south, near Vordingborg?

That she has no idea how many men she's been with?

She's certain they can tell just by looking at her.

2A

He was educated as a teacher, and she used to work as a secretary for an architect.

They are from Iraq and have two children: a boy and a girl.

They live on government assistance.

She cleans at a school, and he works at a fast-food joint in the shopping plaza.

Neither receives a salary, and neither is allowed to take a vacation.

It's considered work experience.

Sometimes she belly dances for him.

On festive occasions they sometimes drink alcohol.

He dreams of moving to Canada, but the children would rather stay in Denmark.

They've forbidden them to hang out at the shopping plaza.

2B

He and two of his old friends have started a small production company.

Business has topped thirty million kroner, and he and his wife have started looking around for a house.

She has nothing against it.

—As long as you keep your hands off the girls, she says.

She works at a hairdresser's down in the city.

She's in her mid-thirties and looks good for her age.

She has long, straight legs and a great ass.

More than once he's offered her a part.

—I'm a nice girl, she says.

—Are you? he says

—Didn't you know?

He trained as a painter but grew tired of painting.

His two friends have a background in IT.

3A

She's seventy-seven.

She and her husband owned a curtain store over on Main Street, but that was more than twenty years ago.

They sold it to an optometrist who sold it to a real estate agent, and now there's a pharmacy there.

That's how things change all the time:

The kids are fired and then find new work.

People she trusted are caught with their hands in the till.

The moon rises over the bog, and suddenly it's gone.

The seasons replace each other.

Only her husband is how he appears: old, half-senile, irritable.

3B

She lives with her mother and her step-brother.

Her father long ago returned to his native Bosnia.

Her brother's father long ago returned to his native Aarhus.

They have a parrot that can talk.

Her brother taught it to say, "Stupid bitch" and "Fuck you, Darkie!"

Her mother has a large, soft rump, and when she gets the chance, she tiptoes to her and presses her face against it.

It feels warm and soft and good.

—Honey, the mother says. What are you doing?

She holds her mother's waist.

She refuses to let go.

—Honey! The parrot says. Honey! Fuck you, Darkie!

Her mother has given up doing anything about it.

4A

He has gotten a postcard from San Francisco.

It's a picture of the Golden Gate Bridge.

It's stuck to the fridge, and every now and then when he walks past it he thinks about a woman he once met at a pub.

She told him that the Golden Gate Bridge was a popular spot to commit suicide.

She had brown eyes and a large soft mouth.

He told her about his relationship to bridges: when the new Little Belt's Bridge opened, he was one of the first to drive across.

When the Farø Island Bridge was dedicated, he was also one of the first to cross.

One time he talked a man down from the railing on Langebro.

—You need to use protection, the woman said. I have herpes.

She left him for a broad-shouldered man from Funen who played center half for KB's first team.

A few weeks later he met a teacher at the same pub.

Sometimes you're just lucky, he thinks.

4B

She can hear when the kids downstairs fight, and when the parrot talks.

On the toilet she can hear all kinds of things.

That also goes for the bedroom.

When the wife upstairs is turned on, she sounds like a cooing dove.

When the husband comes, he sounds like a sea lion barking.

She's lived here for fifteen years and has gotten used to almost everything.

For years she has saved up for a trip to the Galapagos.

She's read a biography of Charles Darwin, and in her eyes he's the most important person since Jesus.

She's worked as a clinical assistant, as a personal care assistant, and for the last few years as a secretary at a school.

She's never been married.

She thinks men are scum.

5A

On rare occasions he greets his neighbors, but he avoids them as much as possible.

He drives a taxi at night.

He believes there's too much traffic during the day, and his theory is that it's because of immigrants:

They all absolutely must have a car, and they've got nothing better to do than drive around and take up space.

He also has a theory about where their money comes from.

He's forty-two.

He never completed his studies in computer science.

A couple times a month, he visits a Brazilian prostitute in the city.

5B

She cleans in a kindergarten on the other side of the bog, and her husband has a kiosk in the city.

They are from Morocco and have lived in Denmark since 1972.

They have four children.

The youngest still lives at home.

The two middle children are doing well.

The oldest drives a taxi and was recently arrested for having eight kilos of hash and three kilos of heroin in the trunk.

He maintains that he didn't know what was in the package.

Her husband goes to the mosque every Friday.

He allows her to work and hardly ever hits her.

Sometimes he kicks the door frame.

Sometimes he shouts.

One time when they watched *Casablanca* on television, tears filled her eyes.

He said:

—An entire film that takes place in a bar?! They should be ashamed! They've never been to Casablanca!

In the elevator she sometimes sees a man in a white suit.

He reminds her a little of the man in the film.

6A

From her window in the living room she can see the bog and most of the houses on the other side.

Among other things, she can see the church and the graveyard.

She and her daughter have been over there to reserve a plot.

They found a location next to the wall.

A rowan tree standing in one of the yards behind the cemetery stretched its limbs out toward them.

She believes it's good if the family has something nice to look at.

She likes the thought of the red berries dropping down on her.

She's begun going to church on Sundays and also to

participate in some of the meetings.

If the vicar is going to say something appropriate about her, shouldn't he have the opportunity to get to know her?

From the kitchen window she can see the shopping plaza and the highway and the low modern houses behind them.

One time when she stood peeling potatoes, she saw a traffic accident.

She quickly called Emergency.

It was snowing, and a long time passed before the ambulance arrived.

A man lay bleeding in the middle of the road.

6B

He has a pistol lying on top of the elevator.

When he needs it, he stands on his tiptoes, pushes the shaft lid off, and fumbles around till his fingers latch onto it.

He's almost been caught many times because someone has got on the elevator, but people don't usually see that the hatch is open.

His address is in Malmø, but he lives at home with his parents.

He owns a black Audi with Swedish plates.

He has lowered the front of the car and installed tinted windows.

He has put lights in the undercarriage.

The police have stopped him more than once, but they haven't been able to bust him for anything.

If his father were to find out what he did, he would kill him.

He has no plans to kill anyone himself, but the sight of a pistol usually forces people to reconsider a bit.

Reconsidering is a good thing, he thinks.

When he meets his downstairs neighbors' youngest kid, he tells him to say hello to his big brother.

7A

During the summer, they sit on the balcony the entire morning.

From here they can see the house on Balzac's Allé.

There's sunshine here.

She reads gossip magazines and he reads adult magazines.

Sometimes they check out a crime novel from the library.

When the children come home from school, they go down to the playground or take a walk around the bog.

They drink coffee, go shopping, and watch television.

They're on welfare.

Ever since a fourteen-foot-tall, double-glazed window fell on him, he has been unable to work.

7B

He's in love with his friend's mother.

She looks ten years younger than his own.

She wears lipstick and eyeliner and tight suits.

She has a Golf GTI.

Usually she comes home around 5:30 p.m., and usually he hangs around hoping to be allowed to eat with them.

She's always friendly to him.

If they pass each other in the hallway or on the stairwell, she looks at him in a slightly questioning way and sometimes touches his shoulder.

She often makes pasta or risotto, and they usually drink wine with their meal.

They eat a lot less than he does, and even though there's plenty of food, he restrains himself a little.

He doesn't want to seem desperate.

He's in tenth grade, and he's always hungry.

He lives with his father.

When his friend talks about the flight attendant across the street, he tells him about an African woman who lives on their block.

He's heard that she's totally hot for young men.

On his way home he usually stops at a fast-food joint in the shopping plaza.

8A

Sometimes, when she's been out jogging, she takes the stairwell up.

It winds in a crooked spiral around the elevator shaft, and on each floor she's reminded of the possibility of selecting an easier way.

She jogs three times a week.

She works full-time and studies at night.

Her boyfriend is a plumber, and every once in a while he asks whether they shouldn't have some kids.

—Look around you, she says to him. Do you really want to have kids here?

He shrugs his shoulders.

—Maybe not.

She's not certain she wants kids at all.

There's so much she'd like to accomplish.

She's recently begun to notice the way he talks.

He says "ferexample" and "bummer."

He can't spell.

Her teacher at the business school wears tweed jackets and light brown Italian shoes.

Sometimes during breaks when she's off by herself he comes over to her to chat.

8B

After they moved to Denmark, her husband began going to the mosque on Fridays.

He demands that she wear a jilbāb and burkha.

He demands that she stay at home.

He prays five times a day and talks about what is halal and what is haram.

There is a Gambian woman who lives in their hallway whom she speaks with now and then.

She's married to a Tunisian and says that he carried on in the same way for a long time.

She says it's because he has too much time to think.

She says it would be different if he got a job.

They've lived at Mosehøj for two years.

They both speak Somali, and the children speak Arabic and Danish at school.

The eldest of the sons is twelve and has a photo of Osama bin Laden hanging above his bed.

9A

He's afraid of Santa Claus.

His parents say that you've got to stay in bed, otherwise you don't get any presents.

They say Santa peers in windows.

There is in fact a little gap between the curtains near the top.

He remains lying in bed until it's quiet in the apartment, and then he creeps into his parents' room.

He can do it so quietly they don't wake up.

9B

She sees him now and then in the elevator or down at the plaza.

During the day he wears dark clothes, at night light ones.

They've never talked.

He looks friendly, but she's not certain he is.

From her window she can see him go down toward the bog every night around 9:00 P.M.

She doesn't associate the bog with anything good.

She knows there was a gallows here once upon a time, and she has heard that bodies were buried at the base of the hill to the right of the path.

A few years ago, a girl from the neighboring block was raped right at that spot.

10A

He's eleven years old, and his hair has begun to turn gray.

His father says that's quite normal back home in Turkey.

He says that's because he'll soon be a real man.

He himself is afraid it's a sign of God's wrath.

He knows it's a sin to celebrate birthdays.

He knows it's a sin to eat pork rinds.

He knows it's a sin to spy on your sister when she's in the shower.

Perhaps the gray hairs are meant as a warning?

His best friend is Danish and lives in one of the villas on the other side of the highway.

They have a huge lawn and a four-wheel drive car.

They eat pork and drink beer.

His friend says he's allowed to have a sip sometimes.

10B

She comes from Gambia.

She's a bus driver, and at regular intervals she has to go to work a few minutes early to put small flags on the bus.

She has lived in Denmark for over twenty years, and there are still certain things that amaze her.

For example:

Why does the television announcer say the same thing every year when Daylight Saving Time begins?

—Tonight at 2:00 A.M. the Danes should set clocks forward one hour.

Does that not include her?

If the Danes are so proud of their democracy, why are they so interested in the royal family?

And why do they call a dictator a king as soon as he's Danish?

She used to be married to a Danish man, but now she lives with a Tunisian.

He's not any easier, but he's more of a man.

11A

He has a hot dog stand in the lot in front of the shopping plaza.

He's had it for fifteen years, and in that time it's just gone downhill.

The more Muslims move in, the worse it gets.

But what else can he do?

He began as a bricklayer, but after a few years with a bad back he had to give that up, and then he got a vendor's license from the county.

The shopping plaza now has a McDonald's, a greasy spoon, and two shawarma takeaway joints.

His wife is a former porcelain painter, and she cleans in a few of the houses over on the other side of the bog.

Thankfully it's under the table.

If worse comes to worst, they'll have to sell some of the hand-painted blue fluted china.

11B

During the summer she bikes through the bog on her way to work.

She doesn't go down there when it's dark.

She's a teacher's assistant and works in a kindergarten over on Ambrosius Stubs Allé.

She can't stand the ducks.

She has read somewhere that they can be both homosexual and necrophiliacs.

A drake can mount the same dead duck eight times in a day.

She's no prude, but *that*, she thinks, is going a little too far.

Bunch of corpsefuckers, she often thinks when she bikes past.

12A

Actually, he has made up his mind:

The silver cigarette case will go to his eldest son.

The small painting from the hermitage will go to his eldest daughter.

His handicapped son will get the television.

The crystal glasses, which were handed down to him by his parents, will go to his Italian daughter.

In truth he could simply leave a list, but it's as if it's not enough.

He believes it should say more, that there should be some kind of explanation or summing up.

He's been married three times.

He lived in Italy for thirty years.

He owned his own company.

He's a former champion Jitterbugger in Copenhagen.

If he were to tell his own story, where would he begin?

He imagines the other regular patrons of The Owl will go to his funeral.

A couple of his ex-wives will probably show up, and perhaps his children will be there too?

The vicar will say something nice about him, and they'll sing a few psalms.

Afterwards they'll drink coffee, and slowly but surely a kind of cheerful glow will spread.

Someone will tell an anecdote.

—He was always good for a round, someone will say.

Or:

—He was always so damn lucky.

Maybe one of the women will shed a tear, and maybe someone will think:

He's the biggest asshole I've ever met.

He'd like to wear the white suit in the coffin.

12B

He's been beaten by the same gang three times, and now he has begun to take precautions.

Every time he goes to the chess club, he takes one of his mother's kitchen knives and sticks it in his bag.

He takes a broad detour around the bog.

A few of them are Palestinians just like himself.

He's in high school and almost never goes down to the plaza.

He has read the entire Koran, and now he has started to read the Bible.

To him there's not much of a difference:

Both are filled with repetitions.

Both are pretty boring.

If he were to choose a book to take with him on a desert island, it would have to be, without a doubt, *The Lord of the Rings*.

13A

Now and then she wakes up when the downstairs neighbor comes home late.

It sounds as if he collides against his furniture.

It sounds as if he talks to himself.

Sometimes he also turns on the television or plays his music loud: usually it's old Danish schlager music.

When she meets him during the day, he's always very friendly.

He's always well dressed.

She is forty-two herself and a Buddhist.

She's happy to live on the top floor of the building.

If you're to minimize the suffering that goes with being human, you've got to detach yourself a little from the world.

She has not slept with a man in eight years.

She has not had a sip of alcohol in ten.

She watches the sun's journey across the sky, and when the telephone rings, sometimes she doesn't pick it up.

13B

He's lived at Mosehøj for four months.

Before that he was employed on a Mærsk tanker ship, and before that he lived at home with his mother.

He likes the view, and the smell in the stairwell reminds him of Mumbai and Colombo and Manila.

He was born and raised in Aalborg.

He's bought a new computer and chats a lot on the Internet.

He was offered a gibbon ape in India, and he regrets not accepting it.

Once in a while he imagines it sitting on his shoulder.

Sometimes he talks to it.

Sometimes it swings on the lamp above the dining table.

He's chatted with a girl in Vester Thorup and told
her about it.

If he gets the offer again, he will no doubt say yes.

SIMON FRUELUND is a Danish author who debuted in 1997 with the story collection *Milk* (US edition 2013). Since then he has published another story collection, four short novels, among them *The World and Varvara*, published by Spuyten Duyvil (2023), and a poetry collection. From 1997 to 2006 he worked as an editor at the publisher Gyldendal. Since 2012 he has taught creative writing at Vallekilde Højskole.

K.E. SEMMEL is a writer and translator. His translations include novels by, among others, Naja Marie Aidt, Karin Fossum, Simon Fruelund, and Jussi Adler Olsen. He is a former Literary Translation Fellow from the National Endowment for the Arts. His debut novel, *The Book of Losman,* was published in 2024. Visit him online at kesemmel.com